SUPERKITTY

HANNAH
WHITTY

PAULA
BOWLES

SIMON & SCHUSTER

London New York Sydney Toronto New Delhi

It was just another normal day at the **Sensational Superhero Agency** in Big City.

I was stuck answering the super phones . . . instead of catching criminals like the crime-fighting kitten I was born to be!

SUPERKITTY

For my husband, Toby.
Thank you for being super. x - HW

For Super Hannah
and the Plum Pudding
Heroes - PB

SIMON & SCHUSTER

First published in Great Britain in 2019 by Simon & Schuster UK Ltd

1st Floor, 222 Gray's Inn Road, London, WC1X 8HB • A CBS Company

Text copyright © 2019 Hannah Whitty • Illustrations copyright © 2019 Paula Bowles

The right of Hannah Whitty and Paula Bowles to be identified as the author and illustrator
of this work has been asserted by them in accordance with the Copyright, Designs and
Patents Act, 1988 • All rights reserved, including the right of reproduction in whole or in
part in any form • A CIP catalogue record for this book is available from
the British Library upon request • 978-1-4711-7509-1 (PB) • 978-1-4711-7508-4 (HB)
978-1-4711-7510-7 (ebook) • Printed in China

1 3 5 7 9 10 8 6 4 2

It was my dream to be one of the Sensational Superheroes.

There's Cheetah – so speedy,

Wildebeest and Lion – so hairy!
Then there's Elephant – so BIG,

and Rhino and Bear – so **strong!**

But they NEVER let me go on their adventures. "Chasing crooks is no job for a cute little kitten!" they always said.

Anyway, it wasn't long before the sensational super phone was ringing again . . .

RING!

RING!

It was Dr Fossil from the Big City Museum.

"**Help!** My latest, greatest dinosaur discovery was supposed to be unveiled today," she cried, "but a terribly, TERRIBLE villain has stolen one of the bones!"

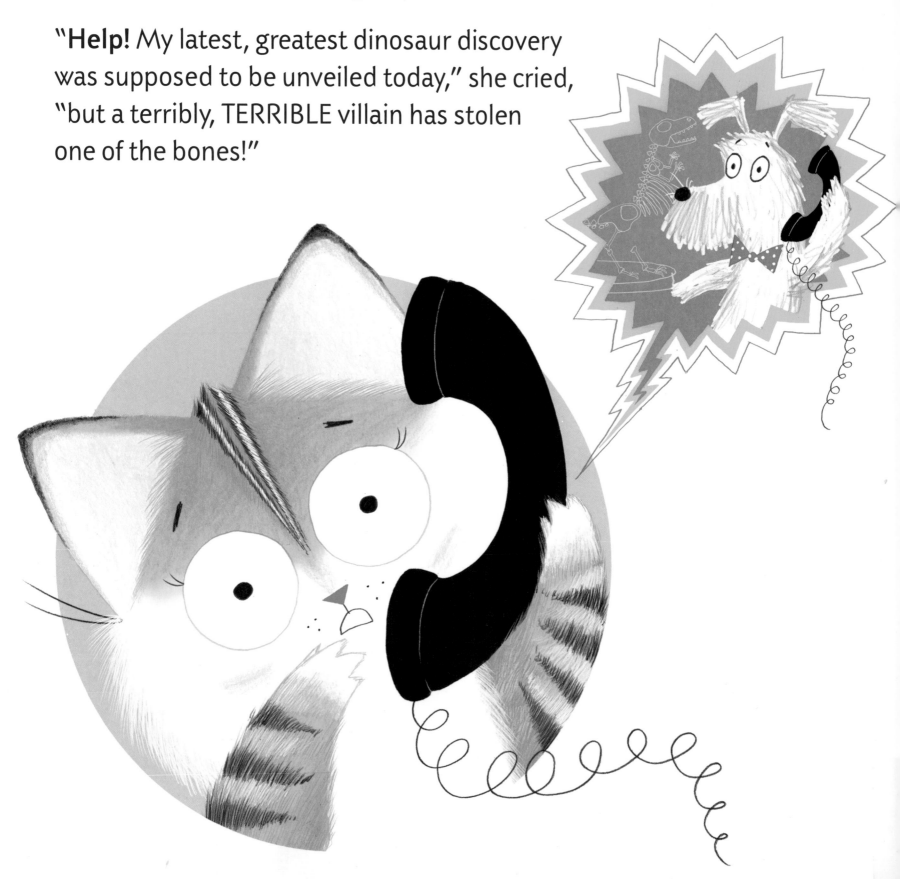

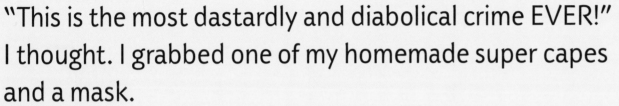

"This is the most dastardly and diabolical crime EVER!" I thought. I grabbed one of my homemade super capes and a mask.

"This time the Sensational Superheroes MUST need my help!"

But . . .

"No, not YOU, Kitty!" said Lion.
"Someone needs to answer the phones!"

"Don't forget to iron our spare capes,"
said Elephant, "and clean out the fish tank."

"Not this time!" I thought. "I'll follow them
and help catch the scoundrel!"

It wasn't easy keeping up with them.
The Sensational Superheroes were SUPER fast!

"There's the thief!" shouted Lion.

"Quick, get him!" said Elephant.

We chased the thief past the bakery.

Bear just had to make a quick stop to refuel his super strength.

We zipped by the hairdressing salon.
Lion and Wildebeest popped in . . .

they said it's important for superheroes
to **always** look their best!

Next we shot across Big City's Big Bridge . . .

that's when Elephant realised it was a delightful day for a swim.

Then we zoomed through Big City Sports Stadium . . .

but there wasn't time to wait for Cheetah to pick up his trophy,

because we had to race all the way to . . .

. . . Big City's SKY TOWER!

Rhino was out of puff.

"Don't worry," I cried, "I'll go on ahead.
We **can't** let the thief escape
with that bone!"

GO KITTY GO!

Claw by claw, I scaled my way to the top and came face to face with . . .

. . . NEFARIOUS NORMAN,

the most **devious** and **despicable** dog burglar in Big City!

"Unhand that bone you dastardly dog!"
I said, trying to sound very brave,
but my voice came out rather small.

"No!" said Norman. He was VERY scary.

"Give me that bone right now!" I said, even though my tail was quivering.

"No," said Norman. His teeth were VERY big!

"GIVE IT TO ME!" I yelled, even though my whiskers were trembling.

Norman came closer. His damp, doggy breath smelled REALLY bad.

"Maybe I wasn't born to be a crime-fighting kitten,"
I thought. "Maybe I am just . . . a kitten."

Norman laughed. "I eat kittens for breakfast!" he said.
He opened his big, toothy mouth VERY wide . . .

then suddenly I had a **brilliant** brainwave!
"Norman," I said . . .

. . . "SIT!"

Nefarious Norman sat!

"Lie down," I said.
Nefarious Norman lay down!
"Now, drop the bone," I said.

Norman looked as though
he REALLY didn't want to.

"DROP IT!" I said loudly.

And Norman did!

"Now roll over, there's a good boy."

That's when the Sensational Superheroes caught up.
"WOW, Kitty!" they shouted. "Will you be our leader?"

We took the bone back to Dr Fossil, who was
so grateful she named the dinosaur discovery
the **Superkitty-saurus!**

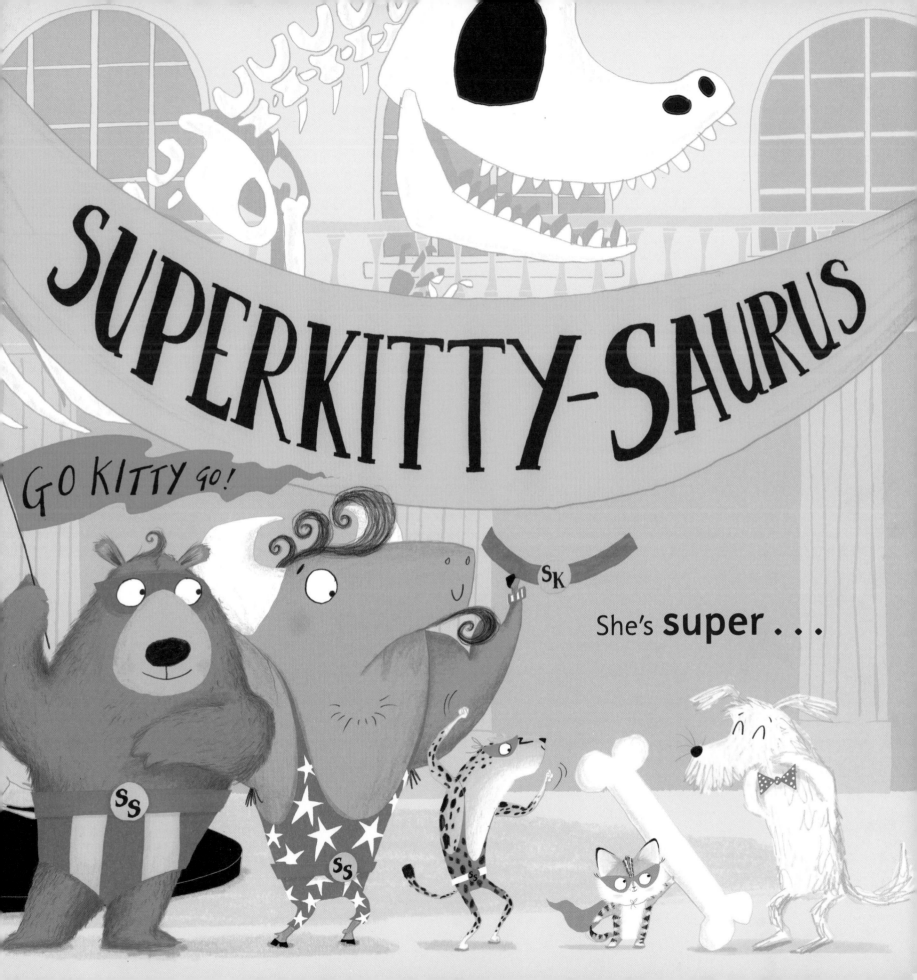

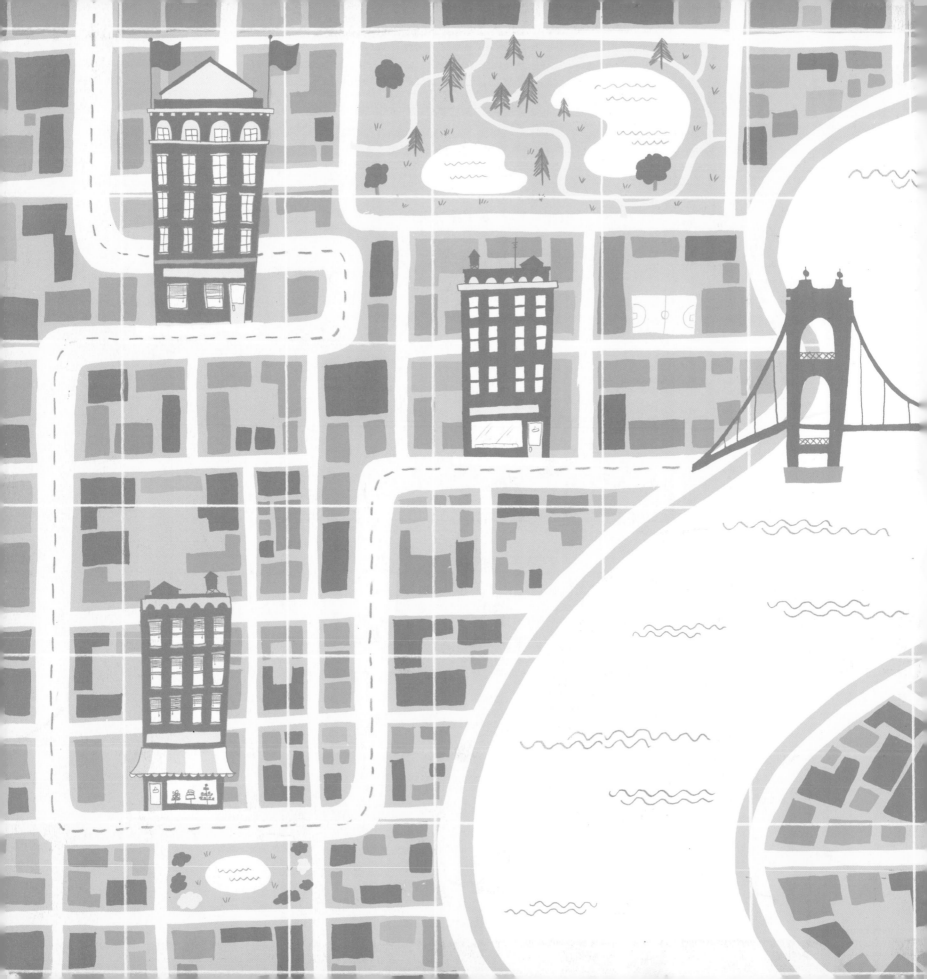